*Weekly Reader Books presents*

# The Pelican And The Peacock

## BY SALLY WITTMAN

An I CAN READ Book®

Original Title: Pelly and Peak

HARPER & ROW, PUBLISHERS

New York, Hagerstown, San Francisco, London

This book is a presentation of Weekly Reader Books.
Weekly Reader Books offers book clubs for children
from preschool through high school. For further
information write to: **Weekly Reader Books,**
4343 Equity Drive, Columbus, Ohio 43228.

Edited for Weekly Reader Books and published by
arrangement with Harper & Row, Publishers, Inc.

I Can Read Book is a registered trademark
of Harper & Row, Publishers, Inc.

Library of Congress Cataloging in Publication Data
Wittman, Sally.
    Pelly and Peak.

    (An I can read book)
    SUMMARY: A pelican and a peacock like surprises but
they like each other better.
    [1.  Pelicans—Fiction.  2.  Peacocks—Fiction.
3.  Friendship—Fiction]  I.  Title.
PZ7.W78444Pe      [E]       77-11833
ISBN 0-06-026559-0
ISBN 0-06-026560-4 lib. bdg.

*For*
*Noah & Emily*
*"If wishes were fishes…"*

# CONTENTS

# TWO SURPRISES

"Peak! Peak!" shouted Pelly the pelican.

"Where are you?"

"I am standing behind you," said Peak the peacock.

"Why are you shouting?"

"I have found something," said Pelly.

"Can you guess what it is?"

"I will try," said Peak.

"Will you give me a hint?"

"Okay," said Pelly.

"I will give you one hint. It is very soft."

Peak sat down to think.

"Is it a rose petal?"

he asked.

"No," said Pelly.

"Is it a raindrop?"

asked Peak.

"No," said Pelly.

"Then give me one more hint,"

said Peak.

"This is the last hint,"

said Pelly.

"It begins with the letter **F**."

"Is it a bit of **F**uzz?"

asked Peak.

"No," said Pelly.

"Is it a scrap of **F**ur?"

asked Peak.

"No," said Pelly.

"You are not even close!"

"Wait," said Peak.

"I have one last guess.

I have been saving it.

Is it a Fish?"

"That is a very good guess,"

said Pelly.

"I wish it were true,

because I am getting hungry.

But it is wrong."

"Then I give up," said Peak.

"Will you tell me

what it is?"

"Look," said Pelly.

"I have found a **Feather**."

"My!" said Peak.

"It is a very handsome **Feather**.

May I have it?"

"Of course you may have it,"

said Pelly.

"Thank you," said Peak.

"Now *I* have a game to play,"

Peak said.

"It is *your* turn to guess."

"Oh, goody!" said Pelly.

"I love games.

What shall I guess?"

"Guess what I will do

with this **F**eather," said Peak.

"Hmmmm…What a hard game,"
said Pelly.

"I will give you a hint,"
said Peak.

"It begins with the letter **T**."

"Are you going to **T**idy up

with the feather?" asked Pelly.

"No," said Peak.

"Are you going to **T**ap

with the feather?" asked Pelly.

"No," said Peak.

"Are you going to eaT it?"

asked Pelly.

"Eat does not begin

with the letter **T**," said Peak.

"No, but it *ends* with a **T**,"

said Pelly.

"And besides,

I am still hungry."

"Wait," said Pelly.

"I have one last guess.

Are you going to play **T**ag

with the feather?"

"No, but you are getting closer,"

said Peak.

"Then tell me," said Pelly.

"Please??"

"Well," said Peak.

"With this handsome feather

I am going to…

Tickle you!"

# TICK-TOCK

Pelly woke up.

He looked at Peak.

Peak was still asleep.

"Today is Peak's birthday,"

said Pelly.

"I will give him a clock

so he will not sleep late.

It must be

a very special clock.

Peak is

a very special friend."

Pelly closed his eyes.

He remembered

a very special clock.

It hung on his mama's wall.

It was a cuckoo clock.

It looked like a tiny house.

In the house was a tiny bird.

Every hour the tiny bird

hopped out and sang

CUCKOO!

One time for each hour.

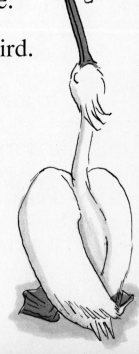

22

Pelly hopped out of bed.

"Goody!" he said.

"I will make a cuckoo clock

for Peak's birthday."

Pelly worked hard

all morning.

Soon the clock was ready.

But Peak was still asleep.

"Wake up, Peak," said Pelly.

"It is your birthday,

and here is your gift."

"Thank you," said Peak.

"Is it a playhouse?"

"No," said Pelly.

"It is a clock.

So you will not sleep late."

25

"Oh," said Peak. "Why is it so big?"

"Because," said Pelly,

"this is a very special clock."

Then he said, "Look, Peak!

It is almost twelve.

Jump back into bed.

Pretend you are asleep."

Peak got into bed.

He peeked out

of the covers.

The hands of the clock

were at twelve.

SLAM! BANG!

The doors of the clock house opened.

Pelly stood there grinning.

He flapped his wings and sang

CUCKOO! twelve times.

One time for each hour.

Then he was quiet.

"How do you like it?" he asked.

"I think it is..." began Peak.

"Is what?" said Pelly.

"It is the funniest clock

I ever saw!" said Peak.

Peak rolled over on the floor.

He was laughing and screeching.

Pelly went back into the clock.

He closed the doors.

Then Peak stopped laughing.

"Pelly," he said.

"I am sorry for laughing.

But you make a very funny

cuckoo bird.

Please come out now."

Pelly did not come out.

30

"Pelly," said Peak.

"You will miss lunch,

and we are having fish soup!"

There was not a sound.

Not even a peep.

So Peak sat down to wait.

CUCKOO!

At one o'clock

the doors opened.

Pelly hopped out.

He flapped his wings

and sang one last

CUCKOO!

Then he went to the table.

He sat down.

"Did you say fish soup?"

he said.

"I will have two bowls, please."

"Sure!" said Peak.

33

"You know," said Pelly,

"being a pelican

is a lot more fun

than being a cuckoo bird.

Cuckoo birds have fun

only once an hour.

Pelicans have fun

all day long."

# BAKING DAY

"I will bake a cake today," said Peak.

"Yum yum!" said Pelly.

"What kind of cake?"

"An upside-down cake," said Peak.

"Will it be

a pineapple upside-down cake,

a peach upside-down cake,

or a cherry upside-down cake?"

asked Pelly.

"None of those," said Peak.

"It will be a plain upside-down cake."

"May I watch?" said Pelly.

"You can help." said Peak.

Peak put on his apron.

He got a deep bowl

and a big spoon.

He put a stick of soft butter

in the bowl.

He added some sugar.

38

Then he mixed until

you could not tell

the butter from the sugar.

He added two eggs

and stirred until

you could not see the eggs

anymore.

He added one cup of milk

and one cup of flour,

a little at a time.

He stirred until

all the lumps were gone.

Then he poured it into a pan.

"When can I help?" said Pelly.

"Now," said Peak.

"Help me turn the stove

upside down."

"Why?" said Pelly.

"That is what makes it

an upside-down cake," said Peak.

"I will help you," said Pelly.

"But it sounds funny to me."

Pelly and Peak lifted the stove.

They turned it upside down.

41

Peak pulled up the oven door

and put in the cake.

He gently closed the door.

"The cake must bake

for an hour," he said.

Pelly and Peak

went outside to wait.

"I will water the flowers,"

said Peak.

"I will read the newspaper,"

said Pelly.

Pelly looked at the newspaper.

The date was April first.

"Now I understand," he thought.

"It is April Fool's Day.

Peak is playing a joke on me.

I will play one back on him."

43

After a while, Pelly got up.

"Excuse me," he said.

"Maybe the cake is done.

I will go and look."

Peak waited.

Pelly did not come back.

So Peak went to find him.

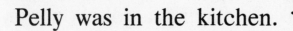

Pelly was in the kitchen.

He was standing on his head.

"What are you doing?" said Peak.

"I am eating a piece of

right-side-up cake," said Pelly.

"A piece of what?" said Peak.

"A piece of

right-side-up cake," said Pelly.

"When I am upside down,

the cake is right side up.

It is delicious!

Try a piece."

45

Peak cut a piece of cake.

Then he stood on his head

and took a bite.

"April Fool!" said Pelly.

"The joke is on you."

"You win," laughed Peak.

"I fooled you first,

but you fooled me last."

Pelly and Peak

ate their right-side-up cake.

Then they stood

right side up

and had a piece

of upside-down cake.

Right side up

or upside down,

it was a very tasty joke.

# A FISH STORY

Pelly and Peak

were at the seashore.

"What a fine day it is!" said Peak.

"I feel so good.

I feel like opening my fantail!

Stand back and close your eyes."

Pelly stood back.

He closed his eyes.

He heard a rattle.

He heard a *WHOOSH*.

"Open your eyes," said Peak.

"RAZZLE DAZZLE!" said Pelly.

"You look like a rainbow!"

"It was nothing," said Peak.

"All peacocks look like this."

"I wish I did, too," said Pelly.

"But pelicans

are not so fancy."

Peak began to strut.

Pelly tried to strut, too.

"I cannot do it," he said.

"My strut is only a waddle!"

51

"Do not be sad," said Peak.

"I will think of a way

to cheer you up."

Peak sat on a log to think.

He jumped into the air.

"Did you get a splinter?"

asked Pelly.

"No, I got an idea,"

said Peak.

"We can go fishing!"

"Goody!" said Pelly.

53

Pelly waddled into the water.

He began to swim.

"You forgot your fishing pole,"

called Peak.

"I never use one," said Pelly.

"Be careful," called Peak.

"The water is deep."

"Do not worry," said Pelly.

"I swim very well."

Pelly dipped and splashed.

"Are you coming?" he called.

"No, thank you," called Peak.

"I hate to get wet.

I will fish from the shore."

Peak put a worm on his hook.

He tossed the hook into the sea.

Then he waited

for a fish to bite.

The sun was warm on Peak's face.

It made him feel lazy.

He shut his eyes

and fell asleep.

A little fish swam by.

He took a bite of Peak's worm.

He pulled.

He swam away

with the worm and the hook

and the line and the pole.

Peak woke up.

"Come back with my pole!"

he screeched.

It was too late.

Peak looked up.

Pelly was waddling

out of the water.

"Oh, Pelly!" cried Peak.

"A fish stole my pole."

Pelly grinned.

He did not say anything.

"Did you catch a fish?"

asked Peak.

Pelly opened his bill.

He dropped sixteen fish

on the sand.

"There were twenty," he said.

"But I had a snack."

"Good work!" said Peak.

"Ho hum!" said Pelly.

"It was nothing.

Fishing is easy for a pelican."

"You see," said Peak,

"we are both good

at some things."

"Yes," laughed Pelly.

"And not so good

at others."

Pelly and Peak went home.

Peak strutted

and Pelly waddled.

But they BOTH felt good inside.